The Thirteenth Year

A Bar Mitzvah Story

THE
THIRTEENTH
YEAR

by Rose Blue

FRANKLIN WATTS | NEW YORK | LONDON | 1977

*The author wishes to express sincere thanks to
Rabbi Paul Kushner, Shoshana Kushner,
Rabbi Baruch Silverstein, and Rev. Henry Wahrman.*

Library of Congress Cataloging in Publication Data

Blue, Rose.
    The thirteenth year.

    SUMMARY: As his bar mitzvah approaches, a
young boy has mixed emotions about its meaning
and how it will effect him.
    [1. Bar mitzvah—Fiction. 2. Jews in the United
States—Fiction] I. Title.
PZ7.B6248Th   [Fic]   76-54273
ISBN 0-531-00382-5

FOR SANDY AND SHLOMO

The Thirteenth Year

Chapter

1

The door of Cantor Michaelson's study was locked. Barry had come to temple straight from school and he was early. He wandered through the deserted halls, past the offices and libraries, and down the flight of marble stairs.

Evening services would be held in two hours. Now the chapel was empty and silent. The early September sun filtered through the stained-glass windows casting midafternoon shadows, but leaving the chapel clearly lit. Barry walked the length of the carpeted aisle and climbed the four steps to the platform. He stood behind the pulpit and looked down. The rows and rows of empty seats stretched before him.

In a little more than two months he would again be standing here, behind this pulpit. The rows would be filled with people, looking at him, listening to him.

It was exciting, but scary. He would be thirteen years old, a man in the Jewish religion, a responsible adult. But now he still felt like a kid a lot of the time, growing but not grown up.

The sound of footsteps behind him startled Barry. He turned and saw Cantor Michaelson walking out of the small room behind the pulpit. The cantor smiled, walked up to Barry, and put his arm around him.

"I didn't mean to disturb you," he said softly.

"I was just standing here for a while," Barry said.

"I know. To see how it will feel."

"I guess I look kind of silly," said Barry.

"No. Not to me. I understand." The cantor looked out at the empty synagogue. "I will never forget the day of my bar mitzvah. I was nearly fifteen."

"Fifteen?" Barry asked. "How come?"

"I was in the camp on my thirteenth birthday," he said. "We weren't allowed to pray. We had to pray alone. To ourselves. And when services were held it was in secret." He paused. "Imagine, it was a crime to pray! Those who were caught would be starved, sometimes beaten. Some were killed. And, along with so many others I missed my bar mitzvah. How we prayed for the day we could live as Jews once again. How we yearned for a real bar mitzvah."

Barry knew that Cantor Michaelson had been

in a concentration camp. But the cantor almost never spoke of it.

"I never knew you missed your bar mitzvah," he said.

"Yes. Finally the day of liberation came. So many were dead." The cantor's face clouded over. "So few left for the liberation. And my own parents were murdered along with so many others. Gone when the troops came to save us." The cantor's eyes looked far away. "My town had a bar mitzvah ceremony for all of us who had passed our thirteenth birthdays in the camp. The largest synagogue in town was filled. People were out in the street. I was so proud to be bar mitzvah at last. Out in the open. For everyone to see. I will never forget that day. Never."

Barry swallowed. "It must have been something to see."

The cantor and Barry left the pulpit and walked silently down the aisle of the empty chapel.

"Do you want to be alone here for a while?" the cantor asked. "Class won't start for fifteen minutes."

Barry nodded and the cantor left, closing the chapel door quietly behind him. Barry sat alone in the last row of the peaceful chapel. He couldn't imagine what it was like to be starved and beaten for being a Jew. He had heard terrifying stories but still it seemed so crazy, so far away, so long ago. Now, when you were thirteen you got bar mitzvah.

You had a party. Nobody ever thought of not being allowed to do it. Of waiting years for the day. Barry tried to picture that scene outside the synagogue of Cantor Michaelson's town. Then he thought back to last spring.

"It's time to decide on a catering place," his mother had said one Sunday morning.

"Almost past time," Dad agreed.

"I guess it will be the Imperial Manor," Mom said.

Dad nodded. "I guess it's time to take Barry to the Imperial and see how he likes it." Dad folded his newspaper and stood up. "Okay. Let's all drive out there now."

Barry remembered the large room filled with linen-covered tables and the workers hurrying around arranging for parties that would take place later that day.

"What do you think, Barry?" Mom had asked.

Barry had looked around the room. "Sure looks like a great place for a party."

"How does a party on Sunday afternoon strike you?" Dad asked. "The day after the services."

Barry imagined the room at night, the lights of the crystal chandeliers gleaming as the people danced.

"Saturday night seems more like a party," he said.

"Okay," Mom said. "Then Saturday night it is."

Barry remembered Mr. Sands, the manager, smiling pleasantly. "Won't you follow me into my office," he said smoothly. "We'll talk about the details." Mr. Sands had silvery hair and looked like an actor Barry had seen in an old TV movie. Barry remembered Mr. Sands saying, "The photographers would be two hundred and fifty dollars," and "three hundred and fifty for the music." He remembered talk of matches and lace cloths and rolling carts.

Now, sitting in the quiet chapel, Barry pictured the big room at the Imperial Manor. It would be his weekend, his party, and it would be very special. Barry heard footsteps and voices outside the chapel. The others had come. He walked out into the hall, now filled with boys. Cantor Michaelson stood with a small group.

"All right," the cantor said. "My second half of November bar mitzvah boys can come into my study."

Barry and three other boys followed Cantor Michaelson upstairs and into his study. It was bright and sunny. The cantor liked fresh air and all the windows were open wide. Each boy sat in the polished wooden chair the cantor assigned to him. A large blue and white book lay on the arm of each chair.

"All right," the cantor said. "You boys have

been studying Hebrew for a long time. Now the day of your bar mitzvah is getting closer.

"Tell me, Jordan," the cantor asked. "What is the main part of every Sabbath and holiday service?"

Jordan fidgeted. "The Torah reading and the haftarah reading," he answered, still fidgeting.

"Good, and do we read any part of the Torah we feel like reading, Carl? Wake up, Carl! Will you daydream through your bar mitzvah, too?"

"No," Carl answered, turning from the window. "Each Sabbath we read a different part."

"Right." The cantor paced around the room talking as he walked and pointing his right index finger at the boy he called to answer his question.

"And what's the difference between the Torah and haftarah, Barry?"

"The Torah is the first five books of the Old Testament, and the haftarah was written by the prophets later on."

"Okay. Now, since the bar mitzvah boy gets the honor of reading the Torah and haftarah for his day, we'll break up into groups. My group will study the last half of November and later I'll coach you individually. You'll find a volume on your chair. That book has the Torah, the haftarah, and explanations.

Barry passed his hand over the shiny blue and white covering.

"I have placed a bookmark in each book," Cantor Michaelson said. "Will everyone please open to the passage I have set aside."

Barry checked for his bookmark and opened to page 93. He stared at the page. His page. He pictured the pulpit of the chapel and saw himself reading the words loudly and clearly as the entire congregation listened in silence.

After lessons Barry walked partway home with some of the boys. Then he waved, and walked the rest of the way alone. He walked slowly, down the quiet streets, thinking. He looked forward to his bar mitzvah, but lately he'd come home and find his parents talking quietly and looking worried. They would see Barry and act as if nothing was happening. Sometimes when he was in his room he could hear them arguing. He couldn't understand it. Until now his parents almost never quarreled. He could count the times he had heard them raise their voices. Now that he was getting bar mitzvah, things were different. Barry was sure of it. His bar mitzvah was causing trouble. Yet this was supposed to be a happy time. Why was a happy time making people fight?

2

Barry opened the front door.

"Phil," his mother was saying loudly, "we've got to start on the guest list. You're not being any help at all. You haven't been much help with anything lately."

"And you've been too jumpy," his father answered irritably.

"Well, there's plenty of reason to be jumpy," his mother said.

Barry walked toward the living room and stood in the entranceway. His parents were silent. Finally his mother said, "What about the tables? We should decide who sits together."

"Ev," his father sighed. "If we took the cards, threw them on the rug, and sat the people anywhere they landed the party would be the same."

"I guess you're right." His mother smiled. "As long as the party is as nice as the other boys' parties."

"We'll do our best," his father said. Barry tried

to tell himself that his feelings were silly, that his parents were probably just excited about his bar mitzvah. But he could feel a worried tone in his father's voice, not the ring of a parent making happy plans.

The doorbell interrupted his parents and they got up at the same time. Barry's dad bumped into him. It was the first time since Barry had come into the room that anyone really noticed him.

"Hi, sport," his dad said, putting one arm around Barry's shoulder. "How are you doing?"

"Okay, I guess."

Barry looked ahead at the large living room mirror near the piano. He was getting to look more and more like his father. They both had sandy hair and blue eyes. Barry had grown much taller in the past year but he still wasn't nearly as tall as he'd like to be. He wondered when he would reach six feet and be his father's height.

"Come in, Papa," he heard his mother say. "How are you?"

"Good. Good," Grandpa said. He put his hand on Barry's arm. "I'm glad to see my grandson."

"Hi, Grandpa," Barry said. "Can you help me with my Hebrew? We learned lots of new stuff today."

"Of course. Of course."

"Let Grandpa sit awhile," Mom said. "Did you have your dinner?"

"Enough for an old man."

"You won't eat anything, Papa? A glass of tea? I have some cookies. You're too thin, Papa."

"Thank you, Evelyn. A glass of tea would be nice. You're a good daughter-in-law."

"What a thing to say. You know you're like my own."

"I know, darling. But you mustn't fuss over me."

"No fuss. I'll get the tea and maybe you'll eat a little something with it."

Barry was always glad to see Grandpa. He couldn't remember any other grandparent. Grandpa lived up the block, all alone, but he would never move in with them. Barry's parents always asked him, but he always kept saying no.

"Two families under one roof is no good," he would say. "And besides, I'm set in my ways."

But Grandpa was always there on holidays. He never missed one. Every Passover, Grandpa was there to take his place at the Seder ceremony. Each Rosh Hashanah, Grandpa was seated in temple beside Barry as they welcomed in the new year together. At Purim, Grandpa would be there, bringing sweets and reading the story of Queen Esther. Each time he read it was like the first time. Fresh and new. Holidays and Grandpa were tied together in Barry's mind.

Grandpa was like a holiday. The time Barry

spent with him was special. And maybe, Barry sometimes thought, Grandpa wanted it to be that way. Maybe that was why he wouldn't move in with anyone.

Grandpa was also always there if Barry or his cousin Leslie needed him. Grandpa loved to read and study. When he worked in the butcher shop he would read in his spare time, but since he retired he spent most of his time with his books.

Whenever there was a problem, you could go to Grandpa's house and he would put down his book and listen carefully. Then he would try to help. Barry's folks would try to solve his problems for him, but Grandpa would say, "What do you think? How do you feel about it?" Lots of times he would tell of an old saying that seemed to help, even though it was written a long, long time ago.

Now Barry turned to Grandpa. "You know, Grandpa, I've been wondering about something."

"What's that?"

"Well, the big party everybody has when they get bar mitzvah. How come everybody does it?"

"Well, times change. This is the way things are done today. But everybody doesn't have to do the same thing."

"What do you think, Grandpa?"

"I think it's good that you are thinking," Grandpa said.

Barry laughed. "Oh, Grandpa. You always give answers like that."

"That's true," Grandpa said and he smiled. "There's an old saying, 'From thinking one may become wise.' Now get your books and we'll study haftarah together awhile."

The thought of studying with Grandpa cheered Barry. It would bring back the good feelings he had at his lessons today.

"Terrific, Grandpa!" he said. Barry ran up the steps two at a time and ran down again carrying his books.

"Let your grandpa eat first," his mother said, placing the tea and cookies on the coffee table.

"A man can sip tea and read his haftarah at the same time, Evelyn." Grandpa turned to Barry. "Now what did you learn today?"

"Cantor Michaelson marked the page for me." Barry opened to page 93. He knew the page number by heart. It was like a magic number. "Here, Grandpa," he said excitedly. "This will be my page."

That Sunday, Barry woke as the early morning sunshine began to light his room. He sat up in bed listening to the noise that had awakened him. For a second he thought it was the vacuum cleaner. But why would anyone be vacuuming now? Barry rubbed his eyes, got out of bed, and sleepily followed the sound. Then he stopped as he saw his father shaving in the guest bathroom near Barry's room. He watched his father run the electric razor up and down his cheek.

"Good morning, sport," his father said. "I didn't see you."

"I was just standing and watching you," Barry said. "Like I used to when I was little."

"I remember," Dad said softly. He walked nearer to his son and ran his hand through Barry's rumpled hair.

Barry stayed quiet for a moment and then looked up at his father. "Is anything bothering you, Dad?" he asked.

"No, no. Of course not, son. What makes you ask that?"

"I don't know. Just a feeling. You never get up this early Sunday morning."

"I just woke up early. That's all. I came in here to shave because Mom was sleeping. Arlene and Jack are coming over for brunch so I thought I'd get an early start."

"Oh, great! I didn't know they were coming over."

"You've been so busy with your lessons you probably forgot. Anyway, I figured I'd drive over to the shopping center before it got crowded and pick up a few things for brunch."

Wait up," Barry said. "I'll come with you."

Barry washed and got into his jeans. Maybe he was wrong, he told himself. Dad said everything was fine. Maybe nothing was the matter.

Barry sat next to his father as the car wound down the nearly empty road leading to the shopping center. "It's so lovely and quiet driving now," Dad said. He laughed. "It sure won't be quiet when the kids come over."

"You can bet on that!" Barry said.

Barry leaned back and let his father enjoy the quiet drive. There hardly ever were any little kids around Barry's house. When he was about four years old his mother told him he was going to have a baby brother or sister. He remembered staying with Grandpa while his father drove his mother to the hospital. They said that when his mother came home she would bring a new baby with her.

Barry's mother was in the hospital a long time, and when she came back she was weak and sick. There was no baby with her, and when Barry asked about his new brother or sister nobody answered him. Barry could remember standing out of sight and catching pieces of adult conversation. "It's awful about the baby," and "Poor Evelyn, losing her parents so young and now this." He remembered his parents saying, "We're lucky. We have our boy." Afterward, when Barry was older he understood that Mom had lost the baby and that she could not have another child.

Barry turned from the window as he felt his father's strong hand squeeze his shoulder. "Hey, Barry," Dad said cheerfully. "Wake up. We're here."

Barry turned to his father, smiled, and got out of the car. He helped his dad pick out three kinds of cheese, some smoked fish, fresh bread, and rolls for Sunday breakfast, and when they got back to the house Aunt Arlene and Uncle Jack were there. Barry always loved to have his aunt and uncle over. Their kids always wrecked the house, but it was fun. Nine-year-old Gloria and eight-year-old Neil were always fighting, while Leslie refereed and Barry helped her.

Barry waved to Leslie. She was out front with Neil and Gloria. Dad went into the house with the packages.

Leslie smiled. "Hi, Barry," she said. Then she turned to the kids.

"Quit that," she shouted. "Do you hear me?"

"How could they not hear you?" Barry said, "the way you're hollering."

Leslie laughed. "I know. But look at them."

Neil and Gloria were pulling at a skateboard, trying to get it away from each other. Gloria, Neil, and the skateboard were rolling all over the sidewalk.

"Now stop that," Barry yelled.

"Now who's yelling?" Leslie said.

"It's mine!" Gloria said.

"It's mine," Neil said. "I brought it."

"You know you weren't supposed to bring a skateboard," Leslie shouted.

Barry ran after the kids but it was too late. Gloria and Neil were tugging at it and running toward the side door of the house. Barry and Leslie got into the house just in time to see Gloria and Neil, standing on the skateboard together, slide into the living room and crash into the couch.

When things finally calmed down everyone sat at the table. Leslie sat near Barry. They were always very close. It wasn't just that she was the only relative his age nearby. She was great.

"How are the plans for your bar mitzvah coming?" Aunt Arlene asked.

"Okay," Barry said.

"It should be quite a party."

"I guess so." He looked down at his plate. "How come everybody has a big party?" he asked. "You can get bar mitzvah without one."

"I guess so," Uncle Jack said. "But most everybody does. Some people seem to think that after all our people have been through, we're entitled to all the celebration we can get."

Leslie put down her fork and sat up very straight. "My bas mitzvah is supposed to be a week from Friday, you know," she said.

Barry took another roll and reached for the jelly. "Sure," he said. "I didn't forget."

"Well, you might as well forget," Leslie said evenly. "I might not be there."

Barry's parents looked stunned. Barry put down his roll. "What do you mean?" he asked.

"The Jewish religion discriminates against women," Leslie announced.

"My daughter, the women's libber," Uncle Jack said with a smile.

"It's not funny," said Leslie. "At our synagogue girls don't get to read from the Torah at their bas mitzvahs like boys do. And did you know the men and women in our synagogue can't even sit together?"

"No kidding," Barry said. "They do in our temple."

"Well, not in ours. And not in some others. Some of the girls are arranging a protest, and we won't go to synagogue anymore if they don't change by next High Holidays."

"Hey, that's cool," Barry said.

"That's why I haven't decided about my bas

mitzvah. I may just have it at home, or not at all."

"Do you hear how she's carrying on?" Aunt Arlene said. She sipped her coffee. "That's why we haven't sent out invitations. Because we've never been sure what our liberated daughter will do next."

"It's my bas mitzvah, it should be my decision," Leslie said.

"Then decide," said Uncle Jack. "Decide."

"I will," said Leslie. "I just need some time to think, that's all."

Aunt Arlene smiled and turned to Barry's father. "Remember when we were kids, Phil? Did we ever have decisions like this to make? What Papa said went."

Barry's dad laughed. "Times change."

"They sure do. Listen, where's Papa anyway? He always comes over when we visit you. Is he okay?"

Dad looked down at his placemat. "Sure, sure. He's just a little tired, I guess."

Mom held out the hot rolls. "Have some more," she said cheerfully.

Aunt Arlene took a roll absently. "Well, we'll stop by on our way home."

Leslie finally decided not to have a bas mitzvah in the synagogue. She said that if she couldn't have a ceremony equal to the boys', she wouldn't have any at all. Instead, she settled on a graduation party, since she had studied her Hebrew.

Barry's mom and dad said that if Leslie was determined to have a bas mitzvah equal to the boys', she could have said so much earlier. They said they were sure she could have found a synagogue to suit her and that she was just being dramatic.

Barry figured his folks were probably right. Leslie acted that way lots of times. She said that if you wanted people to see that things needed changing you had to do something different to "make them sit up and take notice."

Maybe Leslie was kind of dramatic but Barry liked her style. He also liked her party. She had it on the lawn since the weather was still warm. To show that she had learned her lessons she read part of the Torah and haftarah portions for that day. She read outdoors "under the sky, in the open air and sunlight," she said. She didn't chant; she read, part in English so that everyone, even the kids who weren't Jewish, could follow her easily. She did it her way and she did a good job.

Afterward the kids barbecued the franks and hamburgers, put out the paper plates, and served the salads. Everybody helped and everybody had a wonderful time.

"I'm proud of you," Barry told her later. "You

were really good. I hope my bar mitzvah comes off as well."

"Sure it will," Leslie said. "You'll be great."

"I hope so," Barry frowned. "I better be."

Barry was only dimly aware of the grown-ups as their preparations for his party continued. There were talks about the invitations, calls from the photographer, calls from Mr. Sands. He tuned them out at times, like a TV set playing in a nearby room. Like the other boys whose bar mitzvahs were growing nearer, Barry was starting to feel pressured and squeezed. His school homework was more than enough to keep him busy, and the bar mitzvah orientation lessons, growing more difficult as the time drew nearer, added heavily to his work. He began to feel the strain more deeply. It was hard to pay attention to the party preparations as well as his homework and lessons. One day Frank Silvestri rang his doorbell.

"Hey, Barry buddy," Frank said, tossing a football. "Let's get a little practice."

Barry caught the ball with one hand. "I can't," he said, flipping the ball in the air. "I don't have time. There's not enough time for anything anymore. Now I have to finish my homework and go off to my lesson."

"Well, maybe you can take a break and come over after dinner," Frank said.

"I'll try," said Barry, tossing the ball, thinking about how nice it felt. Then he cocked his arm. "Here it comes, the big bomb!" He dropped back and threw a beautiful long pass. Frank caught it on the run.

"Touchdown!" he yelled as he put his head down and ran with the ball to the edge of the lawn.

"I'll see you later," Barry shouted, suddenly feeling much better. "I'll be over later."

When Barry got to the temple, he relaxed in the airy coolness of the cantor's study. He became absorbed in his lessons and enjoyed them. Since his talk with Cantor Michaelson, Barry's studies meant much, much more to him. The lessons were not just words in a book that you recited. They told of the triumphant times and the hard times the Jewish people had lived through. Of the many, many times they weren't allowed to live as Jews. The times of the Egyptian and Spanish inquisitions, the pogroms in Russia, and the horrible times Cantor Michaelson had endured. And now Barry was getting ready to be bar mitzvah. To be a part of a long, proud history. The cantor was narrowing down his group and giving individual instruction during part of his sessions. Each boy had to begin concentrating more seriously on the portion of the Torah and haftarah for his bar mitzvah day.

The hardest part, for Barry, was learning the

haftarah chanting. The haftarah was usually chanted, not just read, and the tunes that were used were very, very old. Old as the old temple in Jerusalem. "These tunes are the oldest tunes in Jewish history," Cantor Michaelson said.

Barry could read music and his singing was pretty good, but the notes of the haftarah were different than any other musical notes. They were little symbols called tropes, unlike anything Barry had ever seen before.

The cantor was sitting with Jordan, coaching him quietly as he kept fidgeting and the other boys went on with their work. Barry kept practicing his chanting. It was coming slowly but he was getting the hang of it pretty well. He chanted softly, trying not to disturb the other boys, and he kept going over and over his chants. He felt a hand on his shoulder, looked up, and saw that the other boys were gathering their books together and standing up. "Hey, bar mitzvah boy," the cantor said softly. "It's time to go home. Remember the old saying, 'Tomorrow is another day.' "

Barry came home and headed for the living room, all set to tell his folks about how well he was learning his chant. Instead, he found them sitting with cards and papers spread out all over the coffee table.

"The invitations are driving me crazy," Mom

was saying. "I don't know how many people we're having."

"It's getting hard to figure," Dad said.

"How come? We just have our family and friends," Barry said.

His parents turned. "Hey, sport," his father said. "We didn't hear you come in. How was orientation today?"

Barry was going to talk about the chants but his parents seemed so busy. "It was okay," he answered. "Why is the guest list so hard to figure?"

"We guaranteed Mr. Sands one hundred people," Dad said. "And we should keep it around that number but it's starting to go way over."

"Why?" Barry asked. "We don't know a hundred people."

"Well, there's Dad's clients in our insurance business. Some of them will expect to be invited. And I do more than work with Dad in the office. I go to organizations to make business contacts and some people will be offended if I don't invite them."

"But I don't know any of those people," Barry said. "They won't even care about how much I've learned. It's my bar mitzvah and I should have people I know there."

Barry thought of the people outside the temple on that long-ago day of Cantor Michaelson's bar mitzvah. Every one of those people cared. Every one of them shared the importance of the day. That's what a bar mitzvah should be. A day that meant a lot to everyone there. An important day of caring and sharing.

"Well, we'll see about who we can cut," Mom said. "We have to decide about the extras, too. Mr. Sands gave us a whole list. We haven't really looked at it. There's champagne-colored linen, and matches and things. We want everything perfect for you."

"We'll have to think about the extras later," Dad said. "Let's get the guest list out of the way first."

"I don't know about your clients, the Greenbergs," Mom said. "If we have them we'll have to have the Grosses, too."

"And the Kaplans," said Barry's father.

Barry walked toward the front door. "I'm going to see Grandpa," he called. His parents said good-bye. They did not look up from their lists.

"Come in. Come in." Grandpa said, when Barry got there. "I didn't know you were coming."

"I didn't think about calling. I just felt like stopping by."

"Since when does a grandson have to call his grandpa. Let me get you something."

Grandpa walked to the kitchen and came back. "I have nothing in the house. Just some toast and milk."

"Is that all you ate for dinner, Grandpa? You always ate boiled beef and roast chicken and all kinds of stuff."

Grandpa shrugged. "What can you do? A man gets older."

Barry plopped down in one of Grandpa's big comfortable chairs. "You know," he said, "it really makes me mad!"

"What?"

"I got home from orientation and all Mom and Dad could talk about was the guest list and the extras. Who cares about that? I don't care about the Grosses or the Greenbergs! I don't care about champagne-colored napkins. What's this whole thing all about, anyway!"

Grandpa didn't say anything for a moment. "Grown-ups are only people," he said. "They do what they think is right and sometimes it isn't right. You're the only child your parents have, so maybe they try too hard. But your parents want you to have the best, and they try to do what's best for you. They're good people, Barry. Look how you're turning out. Remember the ancient saying, 'If you want to know what kind of tree it is, look at the fruit.' "

"Yeah," said Barry dejectedly.

"Come on now," said Grandpa. "Cheer up. Tell me about Hebrew today."

"We're learning our chants," Barry said.

Grandpa nodded. "Good. Good. Here, sit. I'll get my haftarah and we'll study together. Then later we can have a game of chess."

Grandpa walked slowly to get his books. Barry remembered all the walks he had taken with Grandpa. All the bookshops they would stop in and explore. Grandpa loved to browse around bookstores. He would spend an hour in one store, explaining books to Barry. Lately, though, Grandpa didn't go out very much and Barry missed their walks. But he still loved their talks and their chess games.

Barry sat next to Grandpa on the couch, the haftarah spread out on a coffee table in front of them. They sang together, Grandpa singing in perfect rhythm. Then Barry went on singing alone as Grandpa listened. Barry felt warm and happy.

"How was that, Grandpa?" he asked.

Grandpa didn't answer. Barry looked up and saw Grandpa asleep, his head against the back of the couch. He looked very old. It was the first time Barry thought about how old his grandfather really was. More than five times as old as Barry! Barry reached over, gently took off Grandpa's eyeglasses, and placed them on the coffee table. He tiptoed out of the apartment and very, very softly shut the door behind him.

Barry walked down the street quickly and rang Frankie's doorbell.

"Hey, Barry," Frank said. "Come on in. I didn't really think you'd make it."

"I'm taking a vacation tonight," Barry said. "And boy do I need it!"

"How about some Ping-Pong? I'll take you two out of three."

"Oh, yeah," said Barry. "Who says?"

"I say, that's who."

"Since when did you get so tough," said Barry and he gave his friend a playful poke.

Barry stopped to say hello to the Silvestris, who were watching TV in the living room, and followed Frank downstairs to the family room.

They played three games. Barry felt like playing hard, and Frank played a good game. Once Barry returned a serve with so much force that the ball bounced off the table, hit the wall, and was dented badly. They were even at one game apiece and Barry was beginning to feel a little better when Mrs. Silvestri opened the basement door.

"How about some pizza, boys," she called. "I put one in the oven."

"Thanks, Mrs. Silvestri," Barry said. "I'm starved!"

Frank put down his paddle and laughed. "Okay," he said. "Game is called on account of pizza."

They walked up the basement stairs and Barry turned around to face Frank. "Guess I wrecked that ball, Frankie," he said. "Sorry about that."

"That's okay, buddy," he answered. "I'll just put it in hot water for a while and it will come right back into shape."

"No kidding. I didn't know that."

"Sure, heat expands."

Barry laughed. "Too bad everything isn't that easy to fix."

"You're not kidding!" said Frank.

Barry wolfed down his pizza, and Mrs. Silvestri came into the kitchen and smiled. "It's good to see youngsters eat," she said. "I have some pastries I think you'll like."

She put out a tray of pastries, filled a dish, and left the rest on the table. "I'm taking some into Dad," she said, "while we watch TV. You boys eat and enjoy yourselves. There's more soda in the refrigerator."

Barry took a pastry and filled his glass with soda. He wasn't as hungry anymore and he ate more slowly and talked with Frank as he ate.

"Your mom is real nice, Frankie," he said. He looked at his friend. "Tell me," he said. "Do your folks get along okay? I mean, do they fight a lot or anything?"

"No. Everybody's folks fight. But most of the time mine get along."

Barry put his head down. "Mine don't seem to lately. They fight more. And they seem worried a lot of the time. Since they started getting ready for my bar mitzvah."

"Well, maybe they have a lot of plans to make and stuff. My folks carried on a lot before I got confirmed."

"Maybe. I don't know."

"Things will cool down. You'll see. Your bar mitzvah will be great."

"I hope so."

"You know," Frank said. "I've never been to a bar mitzvah before. What's it like? Is it something like a confirmation?"

Barry nodded. "Kind of. The idea is you're an adult and from then on you're responsible for what you do. Your folks aren't anymore. And you're an adult in the Jewish religion. You can be part of a minyan. That means you can be part of all the important prayers. And you can get called up to the Torah at services. That's why you learn the Torah."

"What's so important about the Torah?" Frank asked. "What makes it so special?"

"The Torah is the first five books of the Old Testament, but it isn't like books we get out of the library. It's supposed to be just like the book handed down by Moses. So it's a scroll written on parchment, not regular paper. And every Torah is written by hand in script. It takes eight months to write it."

"Wow. What a job!"

"And sometimes if the person makes a mistake the whole thing has to be started all over again."

"No kidding."

"And you have to learn to chant the haftarah, too."

"What's the haftarah?"

"That's written by the prophets, and it's a special honor to read the Torah and haftarah at services. When a kid gets bar mitzvah he's got the honor of the day. That's why he has to learn it."

"Hey, that's really interesting. I never knew about all that. Now I'll know what you're doing when I come to your bar mitzvah."

Barry finished his pastry and laughed. "I hope I know what I'm doing."

The work went on day after day until one

early October afternoon. School was dismissed at lunchtime so that the teachers could hold conferences with the parents before the first report. The kids were so glad to have a break that they forgot to worry about what the teachers would say to their folks.

Carl had to stay home with his eight-year-old brother and six-year-old sister while his mother went up to school. Everyone gathered at Carl's house. Leslie called for Barry.

"I've got Gloria and Neil today. You're free as a bird and it's not fair, so I came by to ask you to share the wealth."

Barry laughed. "Sure. Which one is mine?"

"Just grab any kid who fights first," Leslie said.

Even though part of the crowd had younger brothers and sisters in tow, there was a holiday spirit in the air. The early fall day was sunny and crisp. The red, yellow, orange, and brown autumn leaves fell from the trees and blanketed Carl's lawn like a patchwork quilt. The younger kids began playing in the leaves, and Gloria said, "Let's build an autumn leaf mountain." The older brothers and sisters helped them and they packed the leaves carefully until a hill was formed, the brilliant colors glinting in the sun. Everyone stood admiring the mountain until Carl's six-year-old brother Lenny and his friend Joe threw Carl's six-year-old sister right in the middle. Little Brenda came up crying loudly and covered with dry leaves. The lovely mountain was ruined.

"Cut that out," Carl said angrily. "Don't you guys do anything like that again. One more time and you better watch out. Now all of you put the hill back together."

"I'll be in charge," Gloria said importantly. "I'm the oldest."

"Okay," Barry said. "You've got the job."

They sat on the grass, keeping an eye on the younger kids and talking. The talk was mostly about bar mitzvahs.

"I have to take care of those kids lots of times," Carl said. "And I don't always have time to study Hebrew." He picked up a leaf and crumpled it. The soft crackling sound was louder than his voice. "My folks are having problems, too," he said softly. "And I have other stuff on my mind." Barry remembered Carl daydreaming at his lessons.

"I know what you mean," Jordan said. "If you've got things bugging you it's rough keeping your mind on everything. But my folks want things right and I can't let them down." Barry thought of Jordan, always fidgeting, never still.

"Your bar mitzvah is first, Steve," Barry said. "Aren't you nervous?"

"Not really," Steven said coolly. "I learned my part. My party is at the Royal Regency, you know."

Of course everybody knew, Barry thought. The invitations said so. The envelopes were lined in red velvet. Steven always acted that way lately. That's why lots of kids called him Snooty Steven. He was tall and good-looking and he knew it. He was rich, too, and he didn't care who knew it. Some people called the Royal Regency the Bar Mitzvah Palace.

"I'm glad yours is first," Jordan said. "Maybe we'll feel calmer after one of us has been through it."

Carl crumpled another leaf. "You know," he said. "We should have a choice. Whether we want a bar mitzvah or not. Or whether we want a party or not. I mean, people decide they want to get married and then they figure what kind of party they want. But when we're thirteen we get bar mitzvah and nobody asks us anything."

"I know," Jordan said. "The whole thing scares me. My folks act like they're having a party for somebody's anniversary or something and I'm just hanging around."

"You're not kidding!" Barry said. "My folks keep going over the guest lists and not asking me a thing. This stuff about extras and guest lists is getting me down."

Gloria came running over. "They did it again," she said angrily. "They're fooling around and they're wrecking the mountain and Joe nearly got hit with a rock that some little kid threw in the leaves. They're not listening to me. I'm the oldest and they're supposed to listen to me."

Barry laughed. "Well," he said. "Try again and get tough. Maybe then they'll listen."

Jordan ran his hands over the grass. "I wish somebody would listen to me," he said.

Carl looked dreamily up at the loosening leaves on the large sycamore tree. "You know what I wonder?" he said. "Why can't we just elope and have a bar mitzvah?"

Chapter

5

Steven did not elope. He stayed for the bar mitzvah that everyone had been waiting for, the first in the crowd. Barry came to the services at 9:00 A.M. as the red velvet trimmed invitations had instructed. A separate section of the synagogue had been set aside for Steven's guests only. There were a number of rows up front, and most of the seats were empty. At first Barry thought he had come too early, but as time passed he realized that the bar mitzvah section was half empty and would stay that way throughout the morning. It was surprising because Barry was sure that Steven would have a huge bar mitzvah with loads of guests.

Barry tried to follow the services, but the guests who were there kept talking among themselves and it was too hard to hear the rabbi or the cantor. The services seemed to go very quickly. Steven's part was much earlier than Barry had expected. Barry hadn't even heard the rabbi introduce Steven. Barry watched carefully and realized that Steven was doing the last portion and haftarah for that day.

Steven stood on the pulpit, smiling, as though he was on a stage. He half-chanted, half-read, and the cantor accompanied him throughout. Steven did no part of the service alone, and from time to time he smiled down at the congregation.

Barry could tell that Steven did not really understand what he was reading. His portion was over quickly and Steven's father was called up. Mr. Roth read something quickly in Hebrew which Barry didn't understand, the rabbi spoke a few sentences, a woman handed Steven a silver cup which he would never use, read the inscription "To Steven from the Sisterhood," and the ceremony was over.

The party at the Royal Regency was Saturday night. Barry had never seen any place like the Regency before. When Dad drove into the parking lot the attendants kept waving him on and Dad kept riding around and around. "It's taking longer to park than it did to get here," Dad said. "This lot must be larger than Paris."

At last the car was parked and another attendant waved them in through a side door. They walked through an endless lobby. A man in a tuxedo stood up front saying over and over, "Which party, please? Which party, please?" Mom told the man that they were going to the Roth's party and he pointed to a stairway. "Up those steps, three doors to the right," he said. Barry looked at the other rooms as he passed and saw two brides and one bar mitzvah boy. The room for Steven's bar mitzvah party was jammed.

"There are so many people here," Barry said. "How come hardly anybody came to the services?"

"Well," Mom said. "It's my guess that the men spent the morning playing golf and the women were at the beauty parlor."

Barry looked around and saw that Mom was right. Most everyone was really dressed up. The men looked tan and the women wore fancy hairdos. Everyone was smiling, talking loudly, and eating and drinking. Uniformed men stood behind the bar serving drinks, and waiters served all kinds of food. There was caviar, meatballs, Chinese-style food, little frankfurters wrapped in pastry, fish, hot and cold dishes of all kinds. Barry couldn't count all the dishes. He had never seen so much food in his life. There was even a marble fountain, with punch flowing from it. People chose their food, took it to tables or stood holding their drinks.

Steven walked around smiling, and acting charming to everyone. He seemed very grown-up and smooth, and a picture of Mr. Sands at the Imperial Manor flashed through Barry's mind. Steven would probably grow up that way, looking important and saying and doing what was expected.

Barry tried as many of the dishes as he could.

He figured that would be the main part of the dinner, but after an hour or so another man in a tuxedo led everyone into a large room. Empty, the dining room was a sea of blue linen. The tables were covered with blue linen tablecloths and lace-edged blue linen napkins.

Barry was beginning to understand what "extras" meant. In case anyone forgot whose party it was, Steven's name was on everything. There were napkins, matchbooks, and menus at every table with Steven Gary Roth written in gold lettering. Instead of the simple skullcaps men were supposed to wear in synagogues, each table had red velvet yarmulkes, with "Steven Gary Roth–Royal Regency" embroidered inside, for the guests to keep as souvenirs.

There were flowers on every table, and at the long table set up for Steven and his friends a big centerpiece of flowers in the shape of a guitar lay on the blue linen tablecloth. Except for the flower guitar, Barry got the feeling that the party was for grown-ups and not the kids.

"This is really something," Frank said.

"Yeah, wow!" Jordan said. "I never saw anything like this."

"Neither did I," Leslie said. "I can't imagine what else anyone could have." She paused. "Though I did hear about a kid in my class who had a belly dancer at his bar mitzvah."

"They've got so many people here," Carl said. "I think I'd freeze."

"You know," Jordan said. "I heard of that once. My cousin Marty told me his friend got so uptight studying and getting ready for the party and all that he just froze and wouldn't go into that room for an hour."

"Well, that won't happen today," Leslie said. "Here comes Steven now."

Barry turned to see the lights dim, hear the music begin, and watch Steven walk into the room, his parents on either side of him, down the long carpeted aisle as though it were his wedding. Steven sat at the kids' table, everybody applauded, and the fruit cup was served.

Barry couldn't believe all the food after everybody had just eaten in the other room. There was fruit cup, liver, soups, salads, roast beef, vegetables —a never-ending stream of food, like a Thanksgiving horn of plenty with a hidden bottom. Waiters served the food at the tables, from gleaming silver dishes, and everything seemed to burst into flame. There were flaming meatballs, and even the roast beef was flamed. During dinner Steven kept smiling, walking around, and saying, "Are you enjoying yourselves?" and "Is everything all right?" to everyone.

Between courses there was dancing to loud music. The talk seemed as loud as the music; and at one point, between the soup and the salad, Dr.

Price, a friend of Mr. Roth, whom Barry remembered going to when he was a little kid, sang "Auld Lang Syne," cried loudly, and was taken from the room for a breath of fresh air. Barry wasn't feeling too well himself. His stomach hurt and the room was warm. He went to wash, and when he dried his hands he saw that the blue towels in the bathroom had "Steven Gary Roth" on them in gold.

At the end a large birthday cake was wheeled in. The band played and relatives were called up one by one. As a musician sang, "Here comes cousin Molly," and "Here comes Uncle George," each relative danced up to the cake and lit a candle until thirteen candles had been lit. Everyone sang "Happy Birthday" and Barry thought the cake was the dessert. But then a huge cart was brought in holding trays filled with all kinds of puddings and pastries. The lights went out and a dish of ice cream was set aflame. Steven told Barry that the dish was called cherries jubilee and the dessert tray was called a Viennese table.

Finally, the guests shook Steven's hand, gave him gifts, and left one by one. Barry followed his father across the parking lot to the car. Dad started the car and edged toward the parking lot exit, slowly, behind a steady line of crawling cars. Barry stared out at the cars' headlights as they moved like one large flashlight across the darkness. He closed his eyes for a moment and woke up groggily as his father pulled into the driveway and shut the motor.

Barry slept late and when he woke he was in no hurry for breakfast. He lay in bed a while, staring at the ceiling and thinking. It seemed that you learned about kids at bar mitzvah time. Jordan was becoming more pressured to do what was expected of him, to be a good boy, so much that he kept fidgeting and moving because nobody ever let him move. And Carl, always looking out of the window, or up toward the clouds, any place but where he was, with his family or at school. And Steven, his bar mitzvah sure helped him to earn the nickname Snooty Steven.

Barry's family stayed home most of that Sunday. Barry did his homework and his parents spent part of the day reading the paper and doing the puzzle together. The phone rang late that afternoon and Barry heard his father answer it.

"Yes," he said. "It's good to hear from you, Rabbi Schecter. Yes, of course, Rabbi. We'd love to come. We'll be there. Thank you."

Barry walked into the living room. "What was that all about, Dad?"

"Rabbi Schecter called. He said the temple was having a special service just for the boys who will be bar mitzvah shortly and for their families. It's next Saturday evening. I said we'd be there."

"Sure," Mom said. "I think that's a great idea."

School and Hebrew lessons took up so much of Barry's time that the week flew by and Saturday came quickly.

The rabbi greeted the Frieds as they walked in.

"I'm so glad to see you," he said. "Cantor Michaelson gave me a wonderful report on Barry's progress. You're raising a fine boy."

"Thank you," Mrs. Fried said. "We're very proud of our son."

The rabbi addressed the congregation for a few moments. "As you know," he said, "the boys here today will all soon be bar mitzvah. That means they will be considered adults in the Jewish religion. They will have the right to be called to the Torah, to form part of a minyan—be part of the service—to fast on Yom Kippur, and fulfill all other responsibilities. This is an important occasion and we are having this family service here today so that everyone may join in. We want everybody to feel something of the spirit that we hope the bar mitzvah boy is feeling and will feel on his day. I will step down now so that the youngsters themselves may conduct most of the service."

The youngsters did conduct the service as the grown-ups joined in. Everybody had some part in the ceremony and the parents seemed to enjoy it even more than the kids.

"As most of us know," Barry said, "the Mincha service is held every day before dark and the Maariv service in the evening. So usually in most temples, as we are doing here today, the Minchah Maariv service is held at the same time, at twilight." Barry stepped down. "Jordan," he said.

Jordan got up, fidgeted a moment, and stood still. He began the Sabbath Mincha service with the first prayer. His voice was strong when he ended the prayer with "Blessed art thou Lord our God, Shield of Abraham." And the congregation answered with a strong "Amen." Jordan looked proud.

The congregation stood, in silent devotion, as each youngster read a prayer aloud. Carl looked straight at the congregation and no place else as he read the closing benediction for peace.

The congregation read responsively from the prayerbook, one person reading a portion, and the rest of the congregation, all together, reading the next portion.

Mr. Fried was called to the Torah, and Barry noticed that his hand lingered on the soft velvet covering for a few moments after he had finished his blessing. There was group singing and everyone joined in on "Ein Ke-elohenu" and some other festive songs.

Afterward the rabbi led the families into a room with movable chairs and asked them to break into discussion groups. Each group was to talk

among themselves about a topic involving Jewish life. There were groups on Soviet Jewry, problems of the Jewish community in this country, the United Nations and Israel, anti-Semitism in the world, and other subjects. Barry's group discussed the Jews in Europe in World War II. Cantor Michaelson was in Barry's group. He told of some of the horrors he had been through in the concentration camp at Auschwitz. Cantor Michaelson rolled up his sleeve and showed a tattoo with numbers on it that he carried with him since that terrible time. "Each time I see my arm, I remember. Nobody must ever forget," he said.

After the discussions the kiddush ending the Sabbath took place. The kiddush was a spread of simple foods—bread and different kinds of salads. At the end of the service a special ceremony was held. The rabbi conducted the blessing of wine, spices, and light, symbolizing fruit, pleasant odors, and the twilight. Mrs. Fried was asked to light the special twisted candle, ending the Sabbath as it began, with a warm, steadily glowing light.

Chapter

6

Barry woke early next morning and went over to Grandpa's to tell him about the Mincha service. When Barry rang Grandpa's bell, Cantor Michaelson opened the door.

"Come in, Barry," the cantor said. "I just stopped in to see your grandpa. I missed him last night. He hasn't been to temple as often as he used to and I miss our talks."

"The cantor and I sit and talk about the Talmud and the law," Grandpa said.

"Do you feel okay, Grandpa?" Barry asked.

"Why shouldn't I feel okay? The cantor said the Mincha service was very beautiful."

"It was great, Grandpa. Everybody did a good job."

"I know your bar mitzvah will be a wonderful day, too," Grandpa said. "I look forward to it so much." He shook his head. "Such a wonderful thing, cantor," he said. "A bar mitzvah."

"Yes. Youngsters today don't appreciate what

it means. I don't know if I would have fully appreciated it either, if it hadn't been for the camp."

"Such suffering," Grandpa said. "Yet suffering often brings wisdom."

"We hope so, Mr. Fried," the cantor said.

"You know, Grandpa," Barry said, "Cantor Michaelson told me all about his bar mitzvah, after the war. There was a ceremony for everyone who missed their bar mitzvahs because they were in the camp."

Grandpa nodded. "I know. Such a beautiful story. With so much meaning. I'm glad the cantor told it to you."

"So am I," Barry said.

Grandpa turned to the cantor. "You should tell the story to more of your students," he said.

"I don't talk much about those times," the cantor answered. "Maybe I should."

"Maybe that's the trouble," Grandpa said. "Maybe we don't . . ." Suddenly Grandpa shut his eyes and gripped the arm of the chair.

"What is it?" the cantor said. "Are you in pain?"

Grandpa nodded. "Dr. Marcus gave me some pills. On the dresser."

Barry ran shakily to Grandpa's dresser and brought him pills and a glass of water. Grandpa swallowed two pills and Barry put the glass on the coffee table.

"Do you need the doctor?" the cantor asked.

"No. The pain will go away soon."

"Grandpa, you are sick!"

Grandpa nodded.

"How sick, Grandpa?"

Grandpa didn't answer.

"Tell me, Grandpa," Barry said. "Please!"

Grandpa paused. "I am very sick. It is cancer and there is nothing to be done. A few months maybe. Time to see your bar mitzvah. But I have lived a long life, done my job, raised good children, and I am not unhappy or afraid."

Barry hugged his grandfather. "Grandpa," he said, "please don't die."

The cantor gently touched Barry's shoulder. "Barry," he said, "the medicine will make him sleep. Let me help him to bed."

Barry took his arms from around his grandfather. The cantor helped Grandpa to his feet and led him to the bedroom.

In a few minutes he came back to the living room. "He'll sleep for a while now," the cantor said.

"Why didn't they tell me?" Barry asked.

"To spare you perhaps. For a while."

"They should have told me."

The cantor put his arm around Barry. "I'll call the temple. I have Sunday school this morning. I'll stay here with you for a while and be late."

"No, cantor," Barry said. "Thank you. But I can stay with my own grandfather."

When the cantor left, Barry called his parents to tell them Grandpa was sick this morning. There was no answer at home. He called Leslie's house.

"I'm alone here," she said. "They left me with Neil and Gloria."

"Leslie," Barry said. "Grandpa's sick. I'm at his house and he got very sick. Leslie, Grandpa's going to die."

Leslie stayed quiet for a minute. "Oh, no," she said over and over again. "Oh, no. Not Grandpa."

"Did you have any idea, Les?"

"No. Honest, I didn't. Oh, Barry. I can't believe it. Being without our grandpa." Barry heard Leslie crying softly. He felt the tears flowing from his own eyes. But he held his breath and tried to keep the sobs inside. He didn't want to make noise and wake Grandpa.

"It's so awful," Leslie said chokingly. "Oh, Barry. It seems like everything is falling apart at once. Everything is so rotten!"

"What's the matter?" Barry asked. "Is something else wrong?"

"Yesterday I heard Mom and Dad talking and business is really rotten. Dad's firm is cutting back all over the place and your father's business is really a mess. Dad said he didn't know what your father was going to do, things are so bad."

"Oh, no!" said Barry.

"I'm sorry I told you," said Leslie, crying. "I shouldn't have said anything, but everything is so terrible."

"It's okay," said Barry. "Don't worry. I'm glad you told me."

Barry hung up and walked into the silent living room. For some reason he wanted to sit on Grandpa's chair. He leaned back and ran his fingers over the upholstery. He remembered sitting on Grandpa's lap when he was a little kid. Here on this very chair.

What would he do without Grandpa? What would they all do? Why hadn't anybody told him? They must have known. Why didn't they tell him?

Barry got up slowly, looked in on Grandpa, and called home again. Mom answered the phone.

"I'm at Grandpa's," he said. "He was very sick, but he took a pill and he's asleep. I'm going to stay with him till he gets up."

"We'll be right there, Barry," Mom said.

Barry walked up and down in front of his parents. "Why didn't you tell me about Grandpa?" he asked angrily. "And about the business. Leslie found out and told me. Why didn't you say anything about that, either? What do you think I am, a little kid?"

"It's your bar mitzvah," Mom said. "We didn't want anything to spoil it for you."

"Spoil it," Barry shouted. "I should know so I could figure out what to do about the bar mitzvah. People should think for themselves. That's what Grandpa always says." Barry looked at Grandpa's empty chair. All of a sudden the tears started and wouldn't stop. "You should have told me," he said between sobs.

"We should have," Dad said quietly. "You're right. But lately we've had a hard time thinking straight sometimes."

Barry looked at his parents. They seemed tired and sad.

"It must be rough on you, Dad," he said, his voice growing softer. "Knowing you'll lose Grandpa."

Dad swallowed and nodded.

"And you too, Mom," Barry said.

Mom reached out and pressed Barry's hand. "It's like losing a second father," she said quietly.

"You know," Barry said clearly. "When you get bar mitzvah you're supposed to face your responsibilities. And that means helping your folks. I'm part of the family and I'm supposed to be growing up."

"It's true," Dad said. "But we wanted you to have a party as nice as everyone else."

"Even though you knew you couldn't afford it?"

"We thought we could swing it. But business has gotten even worse since we rented the Imperial Manor, and Grandpa's medical bills have added to the problems."

Grandpa walked into the living room. "Are you talking about me? I'm the problem?"

"No, Papa," Dad said. "Of course not. We were just telling Barry about our family situation."

"I know. Maybe the boy is right. He should know more."

"Papa," Mom said. "Shouldn't you be in bed?"

"I'll sit up a while." Grandpa walked to his chair.

Barry felt a little better seeing Grandpa in his familiar place. He walked over and sat on the floor near his grandfather. Then the tears came again and Barry rested his head against the side of the chair. He blinked and looked up.

"Grandpa," he said. "Why don't you come live with us?"

"We've been after him for years," Mom said. "You know that. But he's always wanted a place of his own. Even now he won't move in with us."

"I'll get by. I always took care of my family and myself."

Suddenly a scary feeling hit Barry. They were

talking about Grandpa living with them. But where would they be living?

"What's going to happen to our house?" Barry asked his parents. "Will we have to move?"

"Oh, no," Mom said. "Things aren't that bad. We'll definitely keep the house."

"Are you telling me the truth?"

"From here on in," Dad said firmly.

Barry turned to his grandfather. "Then come live with us, Grandpa. You always helped everybody. Can't you let your family help you now?"

Grandpa smiled. "We can learn from the young," he said. "The Bible says one generation passes away and another generation comes."

Barry started to cry again. "Oh, Grandpa," he said.

"Now that's not such a bad thing," Grandpa said. "Don't cry. All right, Barry. You help your grandpa. But help me here. In my own house. I want to be where my pictures and books are, where my own things are, where I am used to being."

"All right, Grandpa."

"But will you be okay here alone?" Mom asked.

"We'll see. For now, I am all right. One thing I know, I will see my grandson's bar mitzvah."

Barry blinked. "You will, Grandpa."

Barry thought of Steven's bar mitzvah, and the

kind of bar mitzvah Cantor Michaelson had spoken of. Grandpa wanted so much to see his bar mitzvah. And Barry wanted it to be right. Right for Grandpa. And right for him. He turned to his parents. "I don't want my party at the Imperial Manor. Honest."

"Sure?" Mom asked.

"I'm sure. I don't want a party like Steven's with everything flaming and more food than anybody could eat and relatives dancing up to light candles on a cake and loud music and everything."

"I know," Dad said. "We didn't say anything, but we don't care for that kind of party, either."

"I wouldn't want that anymore, even if we could afford it. Cantor Michaelson said he remembers the war when there was nothing for people to eat. His cousin who's a rabbi in Lynville now remembers the war in Europe, too. He didn't like the fancy bar mitzvah parties. So he made something called a sumptuary law. He said nobody who was bar mitzvah in his synagogue could have a party with more food than the people could eat. He said if they could afford to throw away so much food, then they could afford to give charity. So anybody who has too big a party has to give the same amount of money to the synagogue for Jewish charities if they got bar mitzvah there."

Mrs. Fried laughed. "That's a great idea," she said.

"Yeah, and Cantor Michaelson said it worked.

You know the cantor was here before with Grandpa and me. We had a talk."

"What did you talk about?"

"Different things. We talked about his bar mitzvah after the war when everyone who missed their bar mitzvah had a ceremony together."

"That sounds like a lovely story."

"It is a beautiful story," Grandpa said. "You should hear Cantor Michaelson tell it."

"That's right. I know you wanted me to have the best at my bar mitzvah. But it's the synagogue service that's important. Not the party."

"You're right, of course," Dad said. "We could see that after Steven's party."

"Then I can drop the Imperial Manor?" Barry asked.

Dad nodded. "I think so. We were to pay half of the entire bill this week. I think there's still time to cancel. We'll lose a small deposit, but it's worth it. Now what kind of party do you want?"

"Just a party with my friends and relatives. People who care about me. I want people who will come to the synagogue to see my bar mitzvah and not go to the beauty parlor or play golf."

"Okay," Mom said. "Tomorrow we'll start a new guest list. Just people who matter to you, and you'll sit down with us and we'll make it together."

"Great! And can we have a party in our house? Right after the services."

"How about a kiddush of cake and wine and some cold salad in the temple right after services?" Mom said. "Then the whole congregation can come. We can have the party for our guests Sunday afternoon. An open house."

"Right," Dad said. "Then if it rains or anything people who are Orthodox can drive over to our house. They won't have to walk from temple on the Sabbath."

"We'll just have a buffet," Mom said. "A few hot and cold dishes and some sweets. We'll make part of it ourselves and order some food from Baron's. They're good and not too expensive."

"That's terrific!" Barry said. "And open house on Sunday sounds great."

"It will be a wonderful weekend," Grandpa said. "And Barry, we must study haftarah together more. There isn't much time left."

Chapter

7

The Frieds started planning Barry's party from scratch. Barry thought of Steven's invitation, trimmed in velvet and mailed in red velvet lined envelopes. "Can we write our own invitations?" he asked.

Next day the family sat around the dining table writing the invitations by hand. It took time but it was fun.

The weeks passed quickly and the mid-November Sabbath morning of Barry's bar mitzvah arrived. The synagogue was filled. Barry didn't want separate seats for his guests. He thought that the whole congregation should be together. The curtains of the ark were opened, and the Torah in the softness of its hand-embroidered covering was carried through the synagogue. The scroll was removed, the rabbi grasped the bottom handles and opened the roll of parchment, and the Torah reading began.

Barry stood on the pulpit, the raised platform of the synagogue, and looked out at the con-

gregation. The people sat looking up at him, in the silent temple, just as he had imagined it would be. For a moment Barry felt as though it might all be a dream and he grew dizzy as an urge to turn and walk down the steps came over him. Then the cantor paused in his chanting and held out a gleaming silver pointer. Barry shut his eyes, opened them, and took the pointer from Cantor Michaelson. The cantor went on chanting and Barry joined him, his voice strong, as the congregation listened and followed in their prayer books. Then Cantor Michaelson's voice was still and Barry chanted alone, leading the congregation.

Barry went on reading the Torah, the portion for that day telling the story of Isaac and his sons Esau and Jacob. He chanted the haftarah for the day, in which Malachi, one of the prophets, wrote of the family of Isaac. The cantor joined in once in a while but he let Barry do most of the chant alone.

For a moment the synagogue was still and the rabbi introduced Barry to the congregation, gave him a present of the Holy Bible, and welcomed him into the Jewish community. Then he called Barry's parents and grandfather up to join them.

Grandpa walked slowly and proudly to the pulpit. Barry blinked back the tears as Grandpa recited the blessing and spoke the traditional prayer of close relatives giving thanks that they have lived to see this day. Then Mrs. Fried spoke:

"We are very thankful and very proud of Barry. A traditional prayer says that we are no longer responsible for Barry, that he is an adult, responsible for himself and his actions. Still there is more to the whole truth than that. We have learned a lot while Barry was learning and we know that we are responsible as a family for what we do. Barry has done wonderfully here today. We're very proud of how he has grown, but he is still growing and we will grow with him."

Mr. Fried kissed his wife's cheek and hugged his father. Mrs. Fried helped her father-in-law to his seat and Mr. Fried turned to Barry. "What your mother has said so beautifully is true. You have taught us a lot as you were studying for your bar mitzvah and getting ready for this very special weekend. You helped us to remember what is important. Barry, you did beautifully. You studied very hard and it showed. We are very, very proud. Now you must go on to remember what you have learned and to use it in everyday life.

"You read today of Isaac, the son of Abraham, the leader of the Jewish people, and of his sons Jacob and Esau. The story told of how Isaac, when he was growing old and thought he had little time to live, learned of the fighting between his two sons and became afraid that there would be nobody to carry on the tradition of the religion. Many of us today feel the same way. We're afraid that our children won't carry on the teachings of the religion and will forget. Your great-grandfather felt that way and so, when your grandfather was bar mitzvah, he gave him his tallis, his prayer shawl, to remind him always of the Jewish traditions. Your grandfather gave me that tallis when I was bar mitzvah." Mr. Fried placed the white, silk-embroidered, fringed prayer shawl carefully on Barry's shoulders. "So now I am passing the tradition of our ancestors to you, with the prayer shawl of your great-grandfather. I know that it will be in good hands."

Barry waited for just a second and then he answered his father. "Thanks, Dad. Thank you very, very much." He fingered the soft silkiness of his tallis fringes. "This is the best present anyone could ever get. And I hope that someday I'll deserve it."

Later, Barry followed the rabbi and cantor as they carried the Torah around the synagogue before it was replaced in the ark. People shook his hand and congratulated him as he walked. Afterward, at the kiddush in the temple, members of the congregation told him how much they enjoyed the services. Barry felt good, and the good feeling lasted all day and into the night. He woke up late Sunday morning to the odors of delicious food and fresh baking. Everybody was up, preparing for the party. He walked into the kitchen.

"Can I help?" he asked.

His mother kissed him. "No," she said. "You can start helping again next week. This is your weekend. You just go and get ready for the guests."

Barry wanted to be together with Grandpa for a few minutes, just the two of them before the guests arrived. He filled a dish with chicken and brought it to Grandpa on the sun porch. Grandpa nibbled on the chicken.

"Look, Barry, a wishbone," Grandpa said. Barry held one end of the wishbone as Grandpa held the other. Barry started to say silently, "I wish Grandpa wouldn't die," and then he caught himself. That wish was a child's wish. It couldn't come true. Barry made his wish and snapped the wishbone.

"You won, Barry! Can you tell me what you wished?"

"That you would be happy this weekend," he answered.

Grandpa hugged Barry. "Then you have already made your wish come true," he said clearly.

By one o'clock the house was filled with the sights and smells of good food and the sound of people talking and laughing. People told him how well he had done and they seemed to really mean it. Everyone seemed to be having a wonderful time.

During the afternoon Barry felt that he wanted to be alone, all by himself for just a little while. He walked quietly out the back and stood on the lawn under the oak tree. Some of the red autumn leaves clung to its branches and others colored the green grass around the trunk. Barry stood there for a few minutes and then he spotted Cantor Michaelson and Grandpa walking toward him.

"Barry," the cantor said. "I didn't know you were out here. Sometimes, since the camp I like to get out to know that I can breathe fresh air whenever I feel like it. Your grandpa needed some air, too." The cantor breathed deeply.

"You did a fine job, Barry," he said. "It was a wonderful weekend."

"I'm so happy and proud, Barry. You did so well. It was such a lovely service. And such a beautiful day for your party, too," Grandpa said.

Barry felt the cool, crisp November air brushing his cheek. He looked up, through the red-dotted branches of the large oak. The sun gleamed in the deep blue of the autumn sky. No clouds covered its warmth. "Yes, Grandpa," he said, "it is a beautiful day."

Next morning Grandpa came over before breakfast, carrying a small bag. "Dr. Marcus wanted me to go into the hospital last week," he said, "but I wouldn't miss Barry's bar mitzvah. Now he has a bed for me and I am ready to go."

"Do you have to go, Grandpa?" Barry asked. "When will you be back?"

Grandpa looked at Barry. "You are a big boy now," he said evenly, "and you want the truth. I may not come back."

"Oh, Papa," Mom said. "Don't talk like that."

"It's all right. I've lived a good life and seen my family make me proud. Don't worry about me. And about business, I've seen hard times come and go. I see the family growing closer and wiser and I know you can make it through this time. There is an old saying, 'The wheel turns,' and things will be better again. Where there is love there's no reason for worry. Now come, Phil, drive me to the hospital."

When Barry went to see his grandfather at the hospital the next afternoon he brought some books for him to read. Grandpa lay in a bed, tubes attached to bottles in his arm.

Grandpa looked at Barry and spoke in a low voice. "Barry," he said. "How good it is to see you. I'm grateful for every moment I am given to spend with my children and grandchildren."

"It's good to see you, too, Grandpa," Barry said softly. "How do you feel?"

"Content, Barry. I lie here thinking about my life and I feel content. Do you understand that?"

"I think so, Grandpa."

"You know, Barry, even though the days left to me are few, I think of the future and my part in it. The part I have given to my children and grandchildren. The part I have had in shaping their lives, in the way they will live their lives from now on."

"I always learn from you, Grandpa."

"Good. Good. That is what Leslie said. We had a wonderful talk before you got here."

"I'm glad."

"And now I would like to talk to you for a few minutes."

"Sure, Grandpa."

"I was so happy to have been spared long enough to see you bar mitzvah. I wanted to see that day so much. And I cannot tell you how proud you made me. How very, very proud." Grandpa paused. "But there is something I want you to remember."

"What, Grandpa?"

"A bar mitzvah is a milestone. It shows how far you've come. But also how far you have still to go. Too many people study for it, then forget, like a test in a school subject that won't matter. But I want you to think of your bar mitzvah as a beginning. A beginning of your life as an adult in the Jewish religion, and as something to grow on."

Barry reached over and pressed Grandpa's hand. "I will, Grandpa." Barry looked at his grandfather. "Grandpa, are you okay?" Grandpa's eyes were open, he was looking at Barry, but he could not speak.

"Grandpa," Barry called. "Grandpa."

A nurse gently led Barry away.

Dr. Marcus went into Grandpa's room, stayed a while, then came out.

"He's getting weaker," Dr. Marcus told the Frieds. "I don't know how he made it this long."

"He wanted to be at my bar mitzvah," Barry said quietly.

Next day Barry went to the hospital after school. He found his parents sitting in the waiting room with Aunt Arlene, Uncle Jack, and Leslie. Barry looked at their faces and he knew. Nobody had to tell him. Grandpa was dead.

Barry sat on the hard wooden bench, the sounds of weeping all around him like a soft stereo. Barry wept quietly and stared at the closed coffin. Grandpa is in there, he told himself. But somehow he couldn't make himself believe it. He had just seen his grandfather. The rabbi who stood near the coffin had stood near Grandpa at the bar mitzvah. It couldn't be. Yet, there were all the relatives weeping, there was the clothing, torn on one side for mourning, and there were the black ribbons in the buttonholes. It was a funeral, Grandpa's funeral, and Grandpa did lie there, in the simple coffin, right in front of him.

"Grandpa." He heard himself crying over and over again. "Grandpa. Grandpa. Grandpa."

The next day Barry still tried to tell himself that it didn't happen. That his parents would wake him and tell him it had all been a bad dream. But the whole family was sitting in Barry's house. Sitting on the hard wooden seats for the week of mourning. There were the covered mirrors, and the friends coming to visit, saying how sorry they were, and bringing food. There was Cantor Michaelson, praying and crying for his friend. And then Cantor Michaelson stood up. "It is time for the kaddish," he said quietly. "We must have ten for a minyan."

Uncle Jack rose, along with Papa and some of the other visitors, to get ready for the prayer for the dead. Barry sat staring at the people. It wasn't real. It couldn't be. And then Barry rose. This was kaddish, the sacred prayer for his grandfather. A minyan was gathering together. And Barry had been bar mitzvah. He was grown now and he had the right to be part of a minyan.

Barry rushed up the stairs to his room and ran back down. He walked into the living room wearing the tallis his father had given him only this Saturday. The tallis his father, grandfather, and great-grandfather had worn. He held it to him as though its nearness brought his grandfather nearer. He fingered the fringes of the prayer shawl and stood beside his father. Loudly and clearly along with the others he joined Cantor Michaelson in reading the traditional kaddish.

"May His great name be magnified and sanctified. May His great name be magnified and sanctified. . . ."

About the Author

Rose Blue is a former teacher in the New York City school system. She was educated at Brooklyn College and did graduate work at Bank Street College. Among her many successful and widely praised novels are *A Quiet Place, A Month of Sunday's, Grandma Didn't Wave Back, Nikki 108,* and *The Preacher's Kid.* Ms. Blue is also a published lyricist and the author of many professional articles.